To all who pick...
–Julia Cook

Duplication and Copyright

Summary: This book teaches children health and hygiene

P.O. Box 22185
Chattanooga, TN 37422-2185
423.899.5714 • 866.318.6294
fax: 423.899.4547
www.ncyi.org

ISBN: 978-1-931636-58-2   US $9.95
© 2007 National Center for Youth Issues, Chattanooga, TN
All rights reserved.

Written by: Julia Cook
Illustrations by: Carson Cook
Design by: Chris O'Connor
Published by National Center for Youth Issues
Softcover

Printed at RR Donnelley • Reynosa, Tamaulipas, Mexico • December 2017

I am a booger. Some people call me a "boogie." I grow inside your nose.

I come in many colors. Most people expect me to be green, but I can be clear, yellow, and even red.

Sometimes I am hard and crumbly. Other times
I am runny, long, soft, and even stringy.

Most people think that I am gross. Some people have even called me a snot! But I don't feel bad about that because I do great things! I keep you from getting sick!! I am a true defender!

When you breathe in through your nose, the air that you breathe in isn't always clean. Sometimes it has dirt and germs in it. Whenever I see a piece of dirt or a germ inside your nose, I swallow it!

If you have more dirt in your nose than I can eat, I call in my booger friends and we have a feast!

When we are full, we want out of your nose because
it gets too crowded for us and you can't breathe.

Since boogers swallow germs, and touching germs can make you sick, you should try to never, ever touch your boogers with your fingers.

The best way for me to leave your nose is for you to blow me into a tissue, throw the tissue away, and then wash your hands with soap and water.

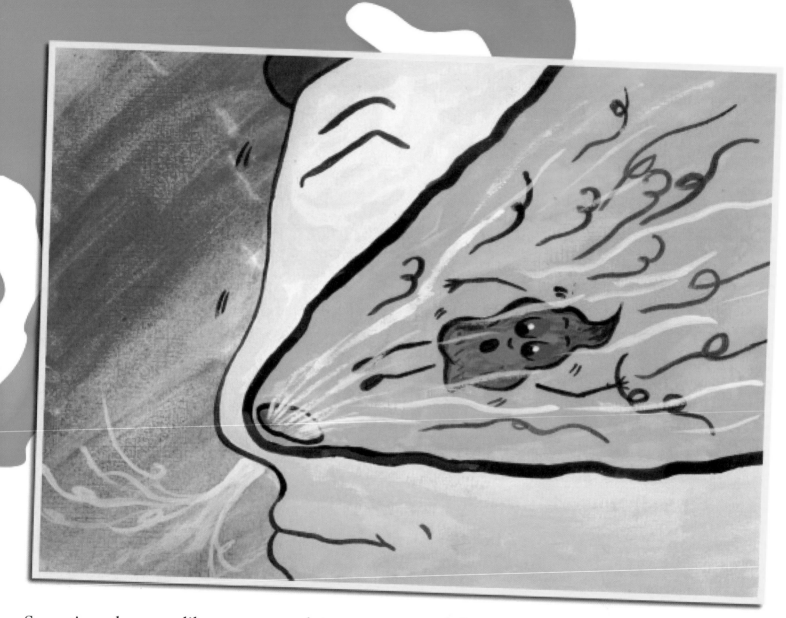

Sometimes boogers like me get stuck in your nose and they won't come out even when you blow really hard.

It's O.K. to use your finger to pick your nose when this happens, but only if you make a "Booger Ghost" with your tissue and your finger like this:

That way, your finger won't get as many germs on it.

If you need to use a "Booger Ghost," it's best to do so in a private place, like in the bathroom, because other people don't like to watch when you pick your nose.

Make sure you throw your "Booger Ghost" away. Then wash your hands with soap and water.

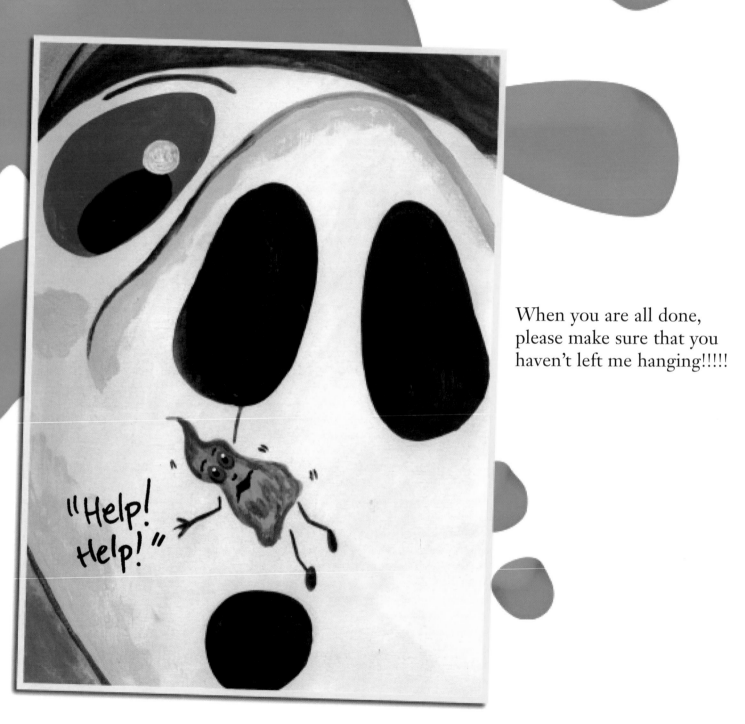

When you are all done, please make sure that you haven't left me hanging!!!!!

Sometimes boogers like me get picked and flicked. Picking and flicking me is very disrespectful. I have worked hard for you and done my personal best to keep you healthy.

If you pick me and flick me, who knows where I will land?

I am full of dirt and germs. If somebody else ends up touching me by accident, I might even make them sick! Then all of my hard work will have been for nothing!

Always remember to treat all of your boogers with respect.
Blow them into a tissue, throw the tissue away, and then wash your hands
with soap and water.

The absolute worst thing that can happen to a booger like me is when you pick me out of your nose with your finger and then eat me!

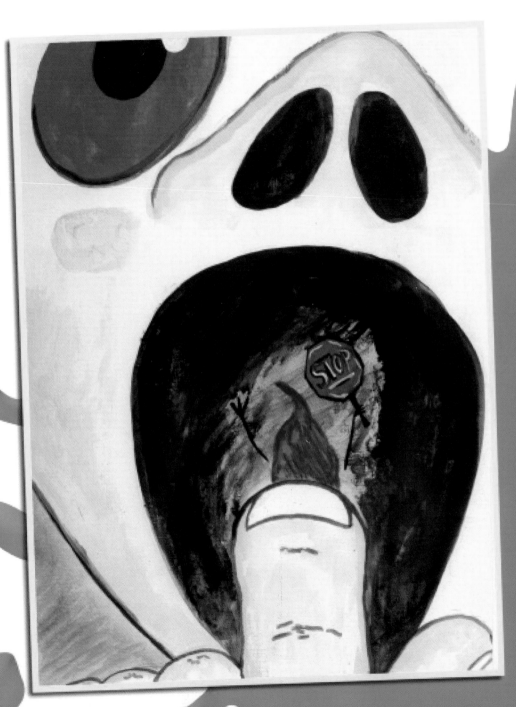

Never, Ever, Ever

eat your boogers! Boogers are full of dirt and germs. Boogers work very hard to keep dirt and germs out of your body so that you can stay healthy.

When you eat boogers... you eat the dirt...you eat the germs!!!

EATING YOUR BOOGERS WILL MAKE YOU FEEL SICK!

When other people see you eat your boogers,

IT MAKES THEM FEEL SICK!

I am a Booger!
I do great things for you.
I work hard to keep
you healthy.
I am a true defender!

Treat me with RESPECT!

Don't pick me without using
a "Booger Ghost."

Don't flick me across the room.

Try not to ever leave
me hanging...

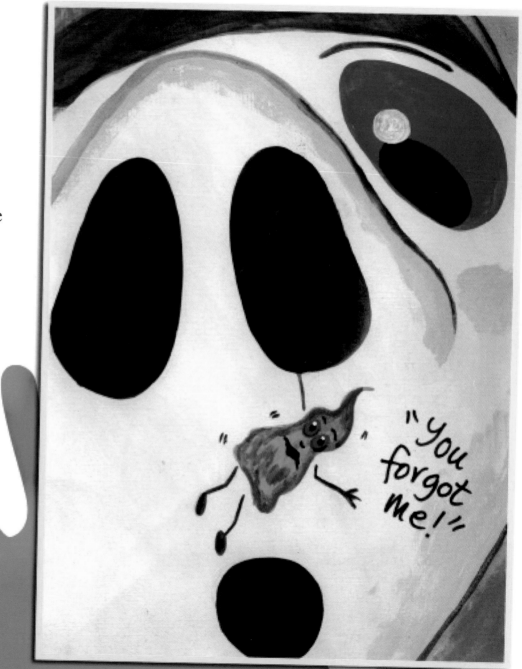

But most important of all: **NEVER, EVER, EVER EAT ME** because eating your boogers makes everyone feel sick.